dick bruna

boris on
the mountain

World International

Boris Bear loved climbing –

climbing up a hill

the hill was steep, but that is why

it gave him such a thrill.

When he reached the hilltop

he had a splendid view

and after all this climbing

that suited Boris, too.

There, the sun was rising

Boris stared at it

there was not very much to see

only a tiny bit.

The tiny bit kept growing

giving brighter light

bigger, bigger, bigger

what a lovely sight.

Just a little later

the sun became quite round

oh, how beautiful it looked

above the soft green ground.

Look, there's someone coming

it was Barbara Bear

with her yellow rucksack

what had she got in there?

Hi, Barbara, said Boris,

I'm very glad you're here

but what is in your rucksack?

the tent, said Barbara Bear.

You see that cloud there, Boris

passing across the sun

I think it won't be long now

before the rain will come.

Oh yes, the cloud grew larger

and others, one by one

came floating up to join it

and blotted out the sun.

We'll go home now, said Boris

turning to his friend

no, Boris, no, said Barbara

you hold the tent this end.

They put the tent up quickly

right there upon the ground

and when the rain came falling down

they kept quite dry, they found.

For Barbara and Boris

although they were so high

were very cosy in their tent –

you might say, high and dry.

miffy's library

miffy
miffy goes to stay
miffy is crying
miffy's birthday
miffy at school
miffy's bicycle

miffy's dream
miffy at the zoo
miffy in hospital
miffy in the tent
miffy at the seaside
miffy in the snow

miffy goes flying
miffy at the playground
poppy pig
poppy pig is sick
boris on the mountain
boris in the snow

"boris op de berg"
Original text Dick Bruna 1988 © copyright Mercis Publishing BV.
Illustrations Dick Bruna © copyright Mercis BV 1988.
Published in Great Britain in 1997 by World International Ltd.,
Deanway Technology Centre, Wilmslow Road, Handforth, Cheshire SK9 3FB.
Original English translation © copyright Patricia Crampton 1996.
Publication licensed by Mercis Publishing BV, Amsterdam.
Printed by Sebald Sachsendruck Plauen, Germany. All rights reserved.
ISBN 0-7498-2995-8

April ~~2000~~

Happy Easter ~~████~~

.love From

Tracey, David and Calum.

X